Your tears fa]

Adukeh the Poet is a London-based writer, poet and facilitator of Yoruba heritage. Her poetry has taken her to many venues, from cookshops and community centres to cathedrals and public squares. Your tears fall like pearls is her debut poetry collection.

Visit adukeh.com to find out more.

Your tears fall like pearls

Published by Hekuda Creative Press, an imprint of Hekuda Creative Ltd, 2025.

© All rights reserved.

Adukeh the Poet asserts her right to be identified as the author of this work under the Copyright, Designs and Patents Act of 1988.

Scripture quotations are from The ESV® Bible (The Holy Bible, English Standard Version®), © 2001 by Crossway, a publishing ministry of Good News Publishers. Used by permission.

Cover design: Adukeh the Poet
Photo: Eve Milner

Printed and bound in the UK.

ISBN: 978-1-068-1666-0-0 (pbk)
ISBN: 978-1-068-1666-1-7 (eBook)

Hekuda Creative Press
publishing.hekudacreative.co.uk

Your tears fall like pearls

Poems by Adukeh the Poet

Hekuda
Creative
Press

*"Sorrow is better than laughter,
for by sadness of face the heart is made glad.*

The heart of the wise is in the house of mourning..."

Ecclesiastes chapter 7, verses 3-4

For Oladeinde Ekundayo

Table of contents

Death came and claimed	1
Grief must speak	2
What it felt like when he made me a cup of tea	4
Widower's lament	8
Quota	10
No kids, no wrinkles — a V&A story	12
The women's group	13
He gazes at my ruins	15
Enough for you	17
Tears fall like pearls I	18
Tears fall like pearls II	20
Gethsemane man	23
He still bears the scars	25
Embrace me	27
Notes	30
Acknowledgements	30

Death came and claimed

Pulled out the tablecloth and left the tray
teacups and cakes
in no disarray.

Yet,
in this
familiar scene

someone
fundamental
is missing.

Grief must speak

Let her have her place
let her tell out her soul
with her calloused knees
and cape of ashes.

Rolling now, screaming then
quietly weeping as
bold faith and
victorious living
shout till
they are hoarse.

Until firm ground caves
and reveals a deeper shaft.
Till the child is lost
and till the memories are stolen.

Until the bright lights,
the bulbs of your dreams
are dropped from a height
into this valley where
only plaintive songs
and sounds can be heard.

Here
let your tears fall
in time with hers.

Allow her arms to settle
around your shuddering form
as you both kneel
under the canopy of dark dust.

Healing begins here.

Make room,
let grief have her place.

What it felt like when he made me a cup of tea

Twitch and tick,
tick and twitch.
Are we only still
when
magnetised to true
home?

Returned,
I shake loose the right key
from its band of brothers and
insert, slide and
turn against a reluctant lock,

the final barrier in my trek to this
North Pole.

You are shockingly present
as I open the door.

Leaning
in the hallway

deep in thought,
keeping warm.

In the Disney version,
your warm embrace gathers me tight–
so tight I can't breathe.

In the fly-on-the-wall version
your hug
is the reply of an absent child
at morning register

truant, but

although you barely move,
I myself
am beholden,
beheld
beloved and
I marvel.

Am I truly the switch
that makes your eyes so brightly lit?
The power now elevating your grooved cheeks?
Shifting the position of your moles on those caramel contour lines?

Now, close together.
Now far apart,
charting a lifetime of,
hidden hills
and un-vocalised valleys.

My heart is flooded;
a winter pitch
before night-time training.

I see clearly what my body
does not receive.
What you do not know how to
give,
I give.

A kiss to
an aged, scoured David,
heavy as marble
you stand firm.

Next, questions domestic arise.

"Have you eaten?"
"What would you like to drink?"
I remove my coat

and enter the
living-and-breathing-and-eating-and
watch-TV room.

The green settee consumes me
like a tasty bowl of noodles.
Plasticine realms claim me
and I descend into the
daughter-shaped place
I occupy for these occasional moments
when it is just you and I.

Was.

Wandering in the wilderness has left me tired,
so hungry,
so ready to receive
what will now be carefully
tucked into
snacks and
mixed
into the brownest of beverages.

Slippers shuffle.
Snap – the kettle's on.

Yawn...
The sound of sluggish water molecules
being shaken, roused, by
rising heat;
they are race-ready in 3 minutes and

poured onto
tea on a string
in a cup.

Light brown sugar follows in (it's good for you).
Milk (semi-skimmed).
The final clink of spoon-in-mug.

Rich tea biscuits accompany
become canapes at this soiree.

My medicine arrives on a tray.

I sip and savour it.
We sip and savour,
drink in liquid life.

Our hearts sing,
our bellies swell.

We sit
and watch
the news.

Widower's lament

Eyes wide
not in disbelief,
but wide with grief
that, roaring lion
raw, serrated iron
scattered,
splintered shafts
arrow sharp
press hard and fast
from what was solid
steadfast.

Our love,
that solid oak tree
sawn
completely in half.

And my, oh my
a hungry sinkhole
devours all above
gasping for love lost to fill
for an end to this.

A suffocating ten-tonne weight
sitting heavy,
full square
upon my sunken chest.

Breathing, make-believing
of normal life;
all the while wheezing,
short of breath
without my life —
my wife.
She's dead.

Like lead
those words on my lips
heard by my head
but not my heart.
That sharp-sighted sloth
still sees her,
still feels her
cries out for her
May!

Come back, come back and heal this pain
let us two be one again,
I am in the grave with you.
You took forever with you,
have taken forever from me.

Gone, so
gone.

You shone then left,
leaving less than half of me here,
eating, drinking, dreaming,
running
from the dark advancing swarm.

How long will I last
till overtaken by our taunting past?

Quota

What is the date, and
when is the time
that
grief meets
its measure?

At what moment
does flow meet limit
and fullness meet capacity?

Does loss know its own measure
as it flows incessantly
with no markers to be seen?

Who can know
if tears will not flow
eternally?

Who knows if
the tank is one
or eight-ninths full?

And yet,
on this day, that month, this time
the quota is most suddenly
unsuspectingly met.

Met when the possibility of
sorrow meeting hope,
sadness meeting joy
seems gone.

The flow shrinks.
Life rehydrates to similar
proportions, if not shapes.

But somehow
a well remains;
ready to supply
the next
quota.

No kids, no wrinkles — a V&A story

You don't have kids do you? You don't look stressed.
Neighbours left dog food on the doorstep.
Once a goat came right into my back garden.
They don't have a Hindu section here — I wanted to learn about Rishi Sunak's religion.
I think he'll do a good job.
We had a good life - I can't complain.
I'll let you go now.

I'm next to a field - sheep and horses and ducks come right up to the bottom of the garden.
I got sandwiches from Waitrose instead.
The coach goes at 3.
£11.50 for a scone and a tea!
57 years we were married.

Walked all the way to Harrods
and got a present for my grandson.
That Boris did a good job didn't he, with Brexit and Covid and everything?
I'm so tired.
I'll let you go now.

You looked friendly.
No wrinkles — I bet you don't have kids!
We never once had a bad argument.
Do you mind if I sit with you?
He would just look at me and say, 'You're probably right dear.'
I'll let you go now.

The women's group

Together
not to fix, but to give voice
to the struggle,
to the fight for wholeness.

Soldier sisters, sharing stories
from the convoluted journey
that leads to liberty.

Heroes in the back room:
admitting weakness,
admitting pain,
admitting slip-ups
into the beckoning arms
of harm, addiction, of death.

Determined and resolute, you come together
again and again and again, and dwell.
To finally face bitter realities,
the piercing horrors that brought you here.

Looking back once again
so you can move forward, free;
to celebrate recovery.

Sitting for a while,
bathing in the silent love of sisters.
Sometimes the tears run,
Sometimes the words rage,

but safely together
you keep pressing on,
through to freedom
with the tender, healing Redeemer.

My weeping warriors, I salute you!
I see your courage, that courage so large;

I see your strength and your strength is so great.

Do you see it?
It's as great as any army,
as great as any platoon.
So never
let your head bow.

Never let your heads bow in shame
as you walk together,
giving voice to the struggle
to the fight
for wholeness.

He gazes at my ruins

I take a look
at this old house
and carry out a building inspection.

Broken bricks
missing tiles
half-hinged doors
and mould.

Then He comes,
and gazes at these ruins.

Brick upon broken brick,
the caved-in roof with missing tiles,
sagging frames clasping half-hinged doors,
towering, tangled weeds.

He gazes at my ruins.

Blurred boundaries
bad habits
tender bruises
broken heart.

He gazes
steadily
at these ruins

with

compassion
and with acceptance

until

I gaze at my ruins;
broken bricks

missing tiles
half-hinged doors

with compassion and,
with acceptance.

And so, I say,

'For all that's less than perfect,
peace, peace be still.'

Enough for you

Thorns in her side and nails in her back,
delivered in brutal tones.

Her china plate heart grew jutting cracks,
nurtured by multiple blows.

This delicate dish, upon it its breaking,
 lay back, looked up, and asked thrice,

"Save me this torture, taking
my breath, my tears, my life.

Fix me, make me glossy, new,
these ugly cracks erase and hide.

For what could anyone do
with a broken plate,
except cast it aside?"

Three times she heard the same reply:
"Bear this broken, sharded state.
My great grace is enough for you
my grace is enough for you."

So, she ceased to ask, to question why
could do nothing but press on and bide.
By and by, do you know, the strength came through
the cracks she tried to hide?

Transformed by what was now joined to this plate
the divine plus the clay, one-to-one, now glued

with shining bright,
golden bonds of grace
proudly on display,
now strong with the bonds of grace.

Tears fall like pearls I

Your tears fall like pearls.
I'll catch and place them in my treasure chest.
I'll store them up until the day
every last one is wiped away.

Then you will see my love for you,
how I was there in the dark
and carried you through.

The cold, the dank, silent blanket of night
brought you into the warmth
into my arms
into light.

You'll gasp in wonder, breath snatched in awe
at the depth of pain, at the vastness of its store,
of pearls and rubies glinting in time,
at how you survived, how I treasured that time.

The bounty will tell,
speaking a language between you and I,
that no other being can interpret
or truly realise.

What the precious gems and stones represent:
a passion deeper than words
a life held and kept
close
tight
and safe at all times.

Though unseen forces
ripped through flesh and heart,
beating core ripped apart
yet still, you are.

A wonder,
a mystery,
alive.

Tears fall like pearls II

Luxury
time with you,

in beauty and stillness, you come, renew.
In the fullness of time you come.
Your presence is warm comfort,
my soul, strummed,
tunes to its eternal home.

Like some hidden passageway passed each day,
my surprise is revived when I see it, and I say

oh!

Oh, it was here all along.
How was I so blind, so wrong?
To turn my nose, lift my chin
to pass answers, warmth, life within.

To think that I could fly high, fly solo
with feathers stuck together
from your very own birds,
stuck together
with your very own glue?

Should have stuck
to you
with you
for you.

But I am here, like you said I'd be
not destroyed, not dwelling in misery.

It will soon be time to open that chest
to wonder at the pearls and rubies. I could never have guessed
I'd have the patience, the will, the determination to see

and then I realise that, of course, that wasn't me
but your strong arms, your life that carried me here,
that stored up each and every one of my tears

and those to come.

So I'll sing with gladness.
I'll flex my hope.
You've helped me to stand
more than cope.

To live, to breathe, bring colour to the day
you've washed my dirty glasses, removed the grey,

lifted the weight that was meant to drown
removed the shard, banished
dark clouds.

You've drawn from the bowl
from the depths of my soul and
exploded it with deep down, genuine
joy.

So when the dark clouds loom overhead
and the lances press deep,
and remind me of what I thought was dead,

I'll cry.

Yes, I will,
but just for a while
in time again I'll return

marvel at how I've survived
how you've come through for me,
came and sat by my side.
Yes,
I'll think of that.

And wordlessly, together, we'll watch the tide
roll in
and out

and in
as the sun sets.

Gethsemane man

What words were whispered in His ear
when overwhelmed by the tides of fear
in the garden where,
overburdened by grief,
to His father, he drew near?

The nauseating truth
struck heart and flesh with pounding fear,
anxiety, anguish and pain to come,
what did the father say
to His trembling son?

What encouragement caused the battle to be won
in the mind of God-made-man?

What vision impelled each step along
the arduous path of this heavenly plan?

What tender words of love wove,
sore tendrils of a rejected heart, alone?

"My son in you I am well-pleased.
I love you,
I love you for doing this for me.
I am with you, I can change your heart and will
put strength and life in you, until,

at daybreak's light, you arise in my glory
your will and mine join hands and go.

You've struggled
until dawn
which now finds you alone,
still but strong,
the shadows gone

the fears now stilled
your face set
to the cross and the joy beyond."

He still bears the scars

Look, up, to the heavens.
Look, up, see where He sits

next to the great throne itself
God's right-hand man.

The beloved son
handed a death sentence, by His
loving
heavenly
Father.

Call yourself a father?

Down Dolorosa way Daddy sent him
struggling under the weight of his death row seat.

"Bend your body and will to self-sacrifice,
pay the otherwise unpayable price,
For the debt of wrongs of every life
trade execution and blood
for gifts of eternal life."

How could he?

Hand the son over to the mockers,
the jokers, the haters,
crowds of fickle traitors,

happy to watch a body
torn to shreds
hang in the sun
until no life or breath was left
till all the blood had run
From the sinless son.
Stripped of pride, strength, and dignity
private organs on display for all to see.

Where's the justice?

"This is the king? The son of God?
Like to see you get out of this one!"

"Messiah? Save the world? You can't even save yourself!
Pathetic."

Hour by hour passed after the midday sun
by nail through bone,
on a cross he hung.

"Where are you God? You've turned your back on me.

That's the one thing I don't have the strength to face
stretched out on this web of pain.

My healing hands scored,
feet twisted and deformed
a crown that claws and embeds my head
I just want to run and find comfort in your arms Dad.

To be free from agony and pain
but instead,
I am brutally,
unjustly detained.

But I did the job Dad, I can't see or feel the joy
but I did it, it's finished."

Yes, that's him.

God's right-hand man,
up there on that throne.

See — he still bears the scars.

Embrace me

Embrace me — your weakness
through me, you can grow
closer to all humanity.

Embrace me — your sickness
grasp my reality and discover
where true health lies.

Lift your eyes to meet mine — your deepest fear
gaze as I shrink
before your very eyes.

Look straight at me — your enemy
peer into my heart,
and find a story that's part of your own.

Forsake me — your vision of a perfect life,
your perfect performance
and find energy, stillness and peace.

Let go of me — your life among the masses.
In solitude, make friends with
the multitude of one.

Walk with me — your pain
I can show you where
to place the balm you need.

Tend to me — your anguish
release your grip on my blade
and let comfort pour in.

Oh carry my weight upon your chest — your grief
I am the measure
of love given, worth lost.

Stay with me — your sorrow,
a salty, healing tide
searing, stinging,
mending
healing in time.

Notes

Earlier versions of many of these poems have been performed at events and festivals.

Gethsemane refers to the garden where Jesus went to pray the night before he was crucified. (See Mark 14:32-42).

Acknowledgements

These poems are centred on my experience of God's love through Christ. He is the one who catches my tears and offers presence, hope and comfort, putting me back together again and again. This book is my thank you.

Jade Nanton and Karina, thank you for giving me the final push to put my poems in book form.

Malisa Ã Elliot and Madeline Zilelian, thank you for your editorial support.

Ian Adams, Liz Evershed, Immanuel Imbang, Tuomo Karjalainen, Richard Lalchan, Rebecca Rocker, and Rita Tam for your advice, comments, and encouragement on the manuscript.

Yinka Ekundayo, thank you for encouraging my writing so much over the years.

Maria Atallah, Miranda Okon, and Yinka Atiko, thank you for your support.

To my mother and my sorority, thank you for all your encouragement, love and support for all I get up to!

www.ingramcontent.com/pod-product-compliance
Ingram Content Group UK Ltd.
Pitfield, Milton Keynes, MK11 3LW, UK
UKHW042111010925
462465UK00004B/6